Where Is Smelly Ann Skunk?

A North Woods Friends Story

Warm wishes,
Chris Thillen

Janet Hill

**Pictures
and Story
by Janet Hill
and Chris Thillen**

*To Gary for your
over-the-top support and confidence
in me, to Candy for your inspiration, and to
Susan for your encouragement. — J.H.*

*To Paul, my guiding light. To Samuel and Peter,
and my sweet memories of reading with you.
To all the Thillkowskis, who bring me such joy. — C.T.*

Text and illustrations copyright © 2019
by Janet Hill and Christianne Thillen
Cover and jacket design by Brad Norr Design

For information concerning the text and illustrations,
please contact Sister Crow Books:
janethillnew@gmail.com or c.thillen2@comcast.net.

ISBN-13:
978-1-7331098-0-2 (HC)
978-1-7331098-1-9 (SC)
Printed in USA

Well now, it was a fine spring day
in the north woods!
Birds were tweeting, honeybees were
humming, and chorus frogs were
singing peep-peep-peep.

But what was Mama Skunk doing?
She was looking for her little girl.
"Smelly Ann? Smelly Ann Skunk!"
she called, "Where are you,
you little stinker?"

When the chorus frogs heard Mama Skunk,
they stopped singing. "Jeepers!" one of them
peeped, "We forgot all about Smelly Ann!"
"Oh-oh!" another frog peeped,
"We were supposed to be watching her!
We have to find her, or Mama Skunk
is going to be so mad!"

The chorus frogs began calling for Smelly Ann, too. They all made so much noise that the other woodland friends rushed over to see what was going on.

Soon everyone was looking
high and low for Smelly Ann.
Where could she be?
Moose and Squirrel checked
the bushes—but she wasn't there.
Beaver and the chorus frogs looked
down by the lake—but they
couldn't find her.

Fox and Rabbit peeked inside
hollow trees and stumps—
but Smelly Ann was not
there, either.

All through the woods,
everyone was calling,
"Smelly Ann! Smelly Ann!
Where are you?"

Then Baby Rabbit looked up and
shouted, "I see her! I see her!
She's up there!"
All the forest friends stopped and
looked up. Sure enough,
Smelly Ann was way up
in a birch tree.
"Mama!" Smelly Ann called.

Mama Skunk looked up.
Her foot went tap-tap-tap.
"Come down from there right this
minute, little missy!"
"I don't know how!" Smelly Ann
cried. Her chin trembled, and a tear
rolled down her cheek.

"Oh, Smelly Ann!"
Mama called to her, "Don't worry!
I'll help you get down!"
"Yes, we'll all help!" everyone
shouted at once.

"We'll all help, but let's think," said Mouse. "What's the best way to get her out of that tree?"

So everyone thought really hard for a while.

"I think I've got it!"
Beaver shouted.
"I can chew on that tree
and make it fall down.
Then Smelly Ann
will come down too!"

"Terrific idea!"
everyone said. So
Beaver sank his long
front teeth into the tree.
But just then Fox said,
"Wait, wait! If you make
the tree come down,
Smelly Ann might fall
and hurt herself.
Let's keep thinking."
"Goodness me! Right you
are!" Beaver said, picking
some bark from his teeth.

They all thought about it some more.
Then Bear said, "Hey, how about this?
I'll climb the tree and carry
Smelly Ann down!"
All the animals thought that was
a terrific idea!

So Bear began to climb.
But when he got halfway up, the tree started to bend.
It started to crack—

Whoa, Nelly!

Bear let go and dropped into
the bushes with a loud crash.

"Oh me, oh my!
What can we do?"
Mama Skunk worried.

Moose looked down
at Bear, who was lying
on the ground. "Ooh,
nice one, Bear!" he said,
trying not to laugh.
"Here's an idea: what
if I stand by the tree,
and all of you get up
on my back and
make a ladder?
Then Smelly Ann
can climb down."

"Terrific idea!" the woodland friends said, and they began to climb up on Moose. Soon they were very close to Smelly Ann.

At the top of the ladder,
Squirrel reached out for her.
Whoops!
Squirrel lost her balance.

They all fell down!
But not Smelly Ann—
she was still up
in the tree,
still holding on tight.

"My stars!"
cried Mama Skunk.
"Not again!"

Well, phooey.
None of their ideas were working.
But the woodland friends
didn't give up.
Nobody wanted Smelly Ann
to be stuck in the tree.
It was getting dark, and they
needed a terrific idea—
really soon.

Suddenly Baby Rabbit spoke up
again. "I know! I know!" she said.
The others looked at her and
wondered how a baby could have
a better idea than the ones they had.
Then Baby Rabbit said, "Fox, please
run and get Grandpa Raccoon,
and ask him to bring us his quilt."

Fox ran through the woods
as fast as she could to
Grandpa Raccoon's house.
She found him playing his banjo
and humming a little tune.

"Help, Grandpa Raccoon!" Fox called, "Smelly Ann
is stuck in a tree. May we use your quilt
to get her down?"
"A-yup," Grandpa
Raccoon replied.
He grabbed his quilt
and followed Fox
to the tree.

Baby Rabbit said to the other animals,
"Now let's all hold onto this quilt
and pull it tight."
Then she looked up at Smelly Ann
and shouted, "JUMP!"

Smelly Ann knew that Baby Rabbit
had the most terrific idea of all.

She let go of the tree and fell . . .

and fell . . .

and fell . . .

And landed—plop! Right in the middle of the quilt!

As the friends all danced around happily, Squirrel said, "Let's have a party! Everyone come to my house, and I'll bake us a nice acorn pie. We all helped today." "Yes," Fox agreed, "Baby Rabbit is as smart as she can be, and all of us showed Smelly Ann that we care about her very much."

At the party, the friends ate acorn pie,
pinecone cookies, and brambleberry cake.
They helped themselves to fiddlehead stew.
They were all so happy that Smelly Ann
was safe.

And what did Mama Skunk do after the party? She wrapped Smelly Ann in her arms, and the two of them snuggled for a long, long time.

Yessiree, it was a fine spring day for all the friends in the north woods! As the moon came up, the chorus frogs sang for joy.

Peep! Peep! Peep!
Smelly Ann's asleep!
We're all so glad
her mom's not mad!
Peep! Peep! Peep!